Dianne Stewart was born and brought up in Natal, South Africa, where she still lives. After high school, she studied psychology and then African languages so that she could communicate with the people around her in their own languages. Several of her books have been translated into Xhosa and Zulu. *The Gift of the Sun* was chosen as one of Child Education's Best Books of 1996. Dianne's second book for Frances Lincoln is *The Dove.*

Jude Daly lives in Cape Town, South Africa with her husband, writer and illustrator Niki Daly, and their sons Joe and Leo. Her previous titles for Frances Lincoln include *The Dove*, also written by Dianne Stewart, her own retelling of an Irish Cinderella story entitled *Fair, Brown and Trembling* and *The Elephant's Pillow*, written by Diana Reynolds Roome, which was awarded a U.S. Fall 2003 Parents' Choice Silver Honor. Jude's latest book is *To Every Thing There is a Season.*

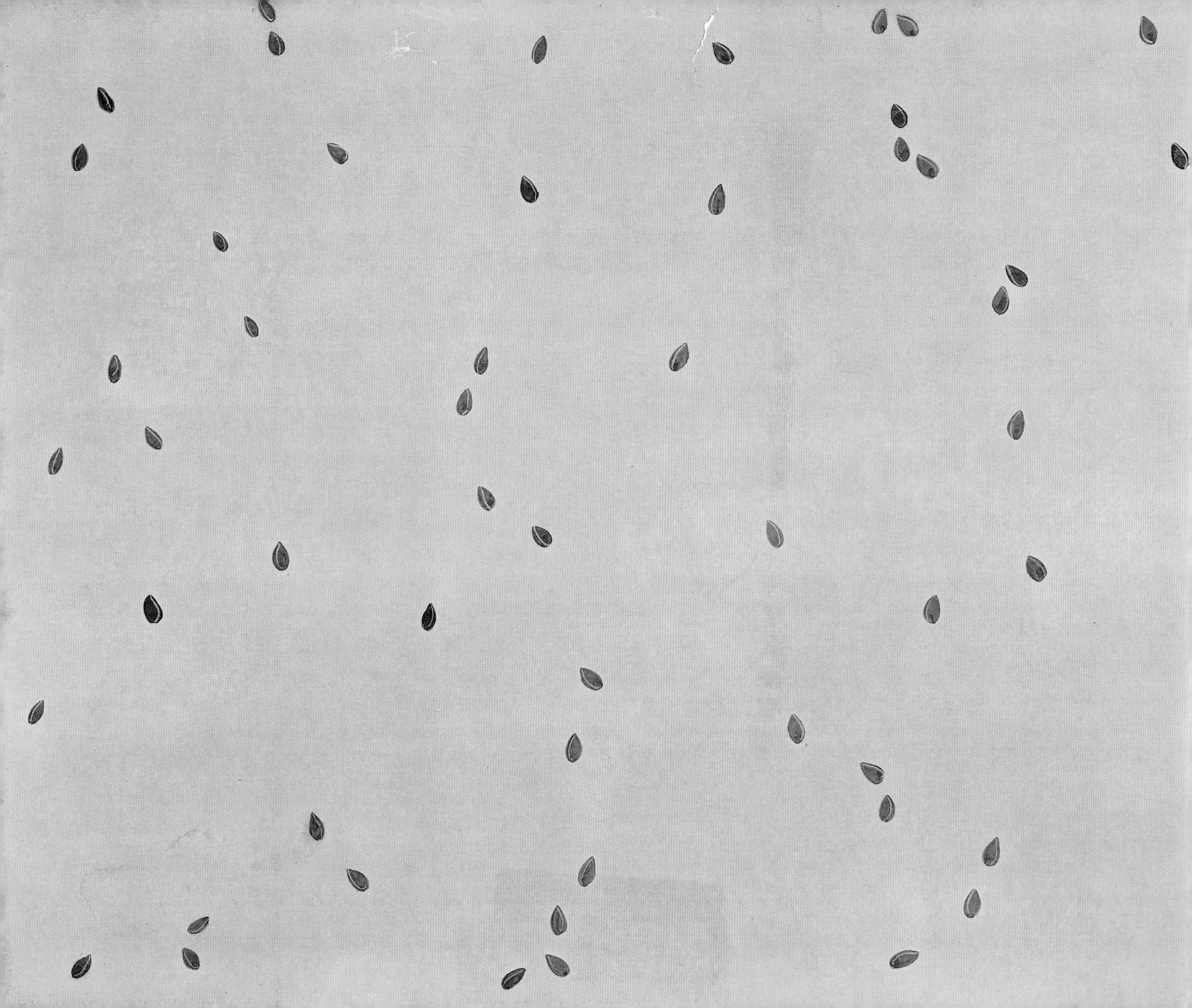

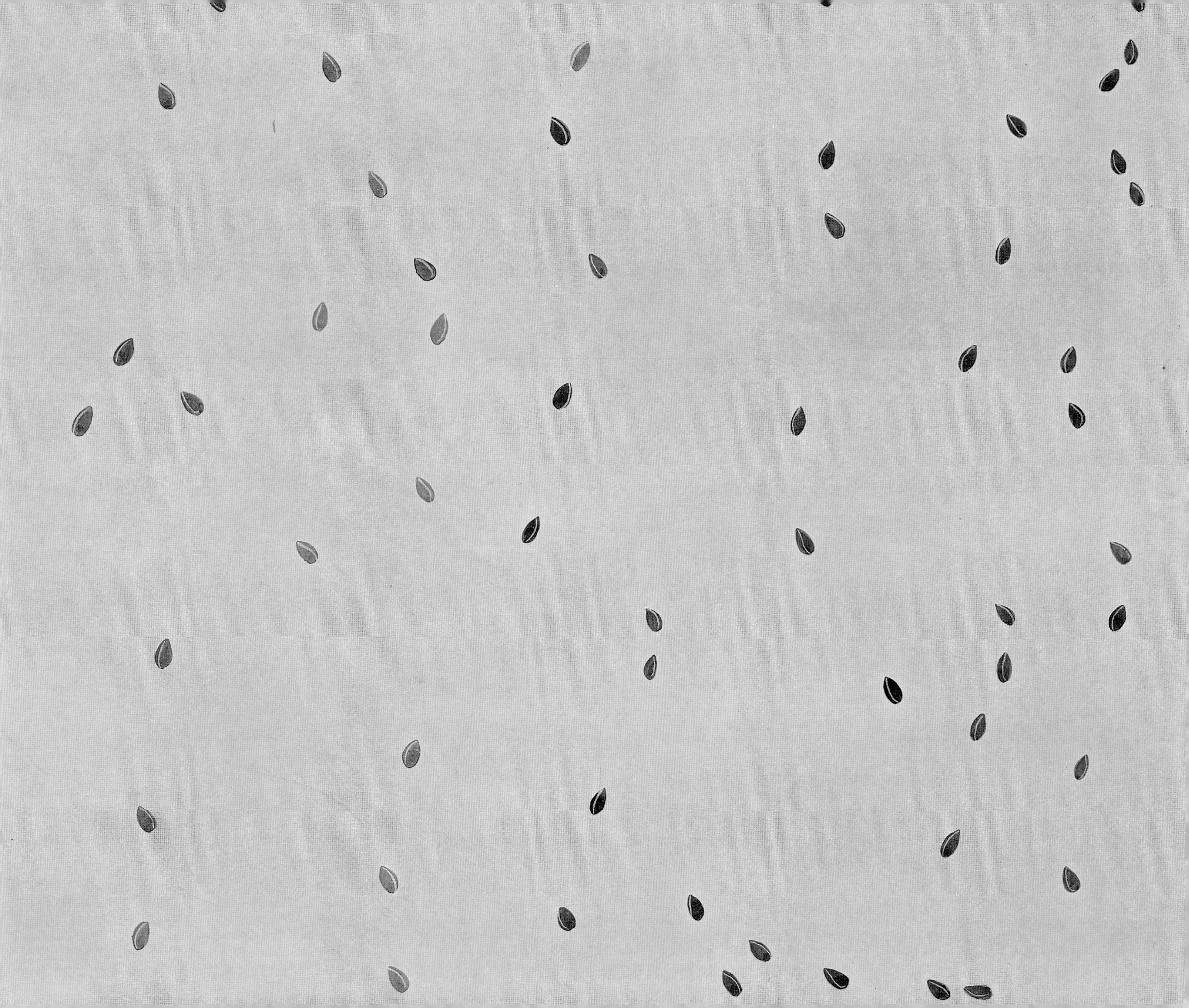

For Lauren, with my love ☼ D.S.

For my mother, with love ☼ J.D.

By arrangement with The Inkman, Cape Town, South Africa

First published in Great Britain in 1996 by
Frances Lincoln Children's Books, 4 Torriano Mews,
Torriano Avenue, London NW5 2RZ
www.franceslincoln.com

Distributed in the USA by Publishers Group West

This paperback edition first published in Great Britain and the USA in 2007

British Library Cataloguing in Publication Data available on request

ISBN 978-1-84507-787-7

Set in Bembo

Printed in China

3 5 7 9 8 6 4

THE GIFT OF THE SUN

A TALE FROM SOUTH AFRICA

Dianne Stewart • *Illustrated by* Jude Daly

F
FRANCES LINCOLN
CHILDREN'S BOOKS

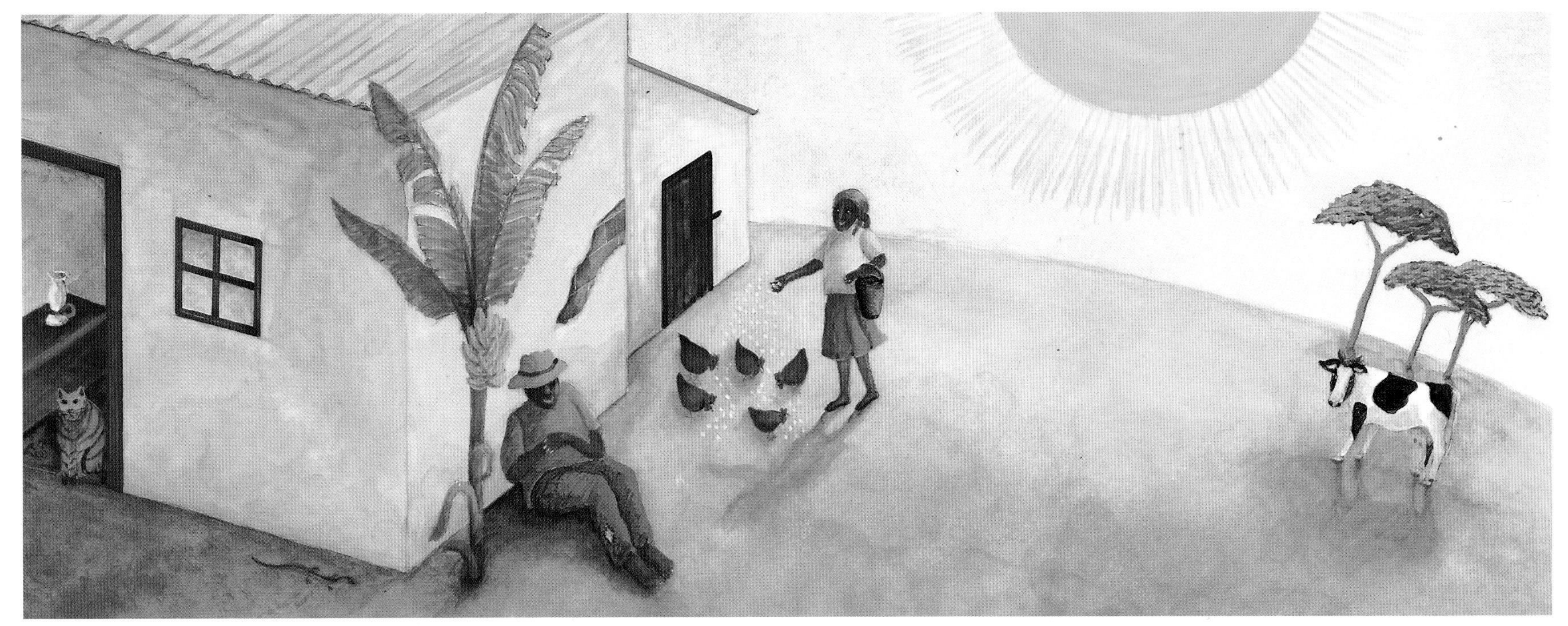

Thulani loved to bask all day in the sun.

Every afternoon when the sun began to sink, he stood up, straightened his stiff back and went to milk the cow.

One day, as he was milking, Thulani said, "I am tired of all this milking. I will sell the cow and buy a goat."

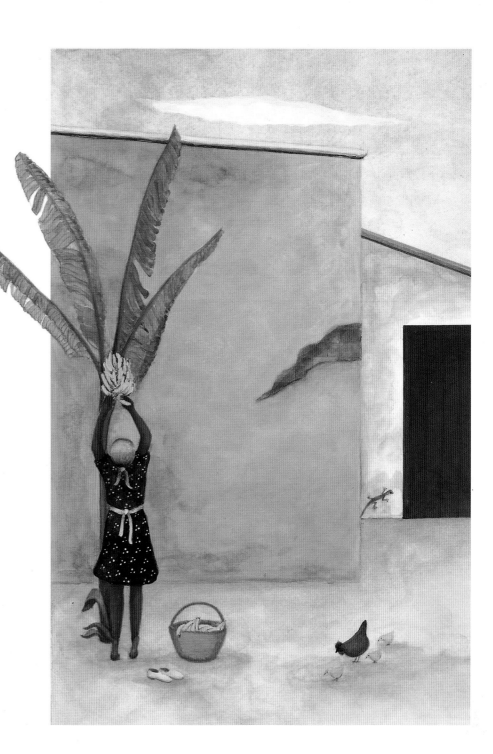

Early next morning, Thulani left the house with his cow and returned at midday, led by a grizzly old billy-goat.

"Oh Thulani!" sighed Dora, his wife. "You've sold the cow and now we'll have no milk! What good is this goat to us?"

"Goats can look after themselves, Dora," said Thulani.

Dora turned away and went to pick bananas.

Thulani went back to his life in the sun - until one day the goat strayed into the house and ate their store of dried corn.

"Wake up, Thulani!" shouted Dora. "That nuisance goat has eaten all our seed. It will have to go!"

Thulani felt sad. But that night he had an idea. "I will sell the goat and buy a sheep," he thought.

The next morning, while the dew was still on the ground, Thulani left the house with the old billy-goat. He came back that evening, just as the horns of the crescent moon were rising through the wood-smoke.

“Where have you been?” cried Dora.

“To the store,” said Thulani. “I’ve bought you a sheep. She won’t be any trouble.”

Dora shrugged her shoulders. “At least we’ll be able to sell her fleece in the spring,” she said.

All winter long, Thulani sat about, looking after the sheep. He missed being able to sleep in the sun.

When the first leaves appeared on the trees, Dora said,

"That sheep looks shaggy. It's time to shear her."

Thulani brought out the shears and started to clip the sheep. But as he was shearing, he thought, "This work is too much for me. I will sell the fleece *and* the sheep."

The next day, Thulani left the house with the sheep and the shaggy fleece. He sold them at the store, and bought three geese with the money.

"Dora will be pleased," Thulani thought, as he drove the geese home. "Geese eat anything."

But when Dora saw them, she said, "Thulani, we need seed, not geese. It is spring and time to plant our crops. Don't you remember - that nuisance goat ate all our seed?"

So next morning, poor Thulani left the house with the three geese, went back to the store, and exchanged them for some seed.

All the way home, the seeds jumped around in Thulani's pocket. "At last," he thought, "Dora will be pleased with me."

He looked at the ground that Dora had prepared. "I'll do the planting," he said. "I'll start today."

And as he sowed the seed, he looked up and saw the first swallows flitting overhead. Summer was coming. He could bask in the sun once more!

SPECIALS
WANTED
FRESH EGGS
UBUNTU

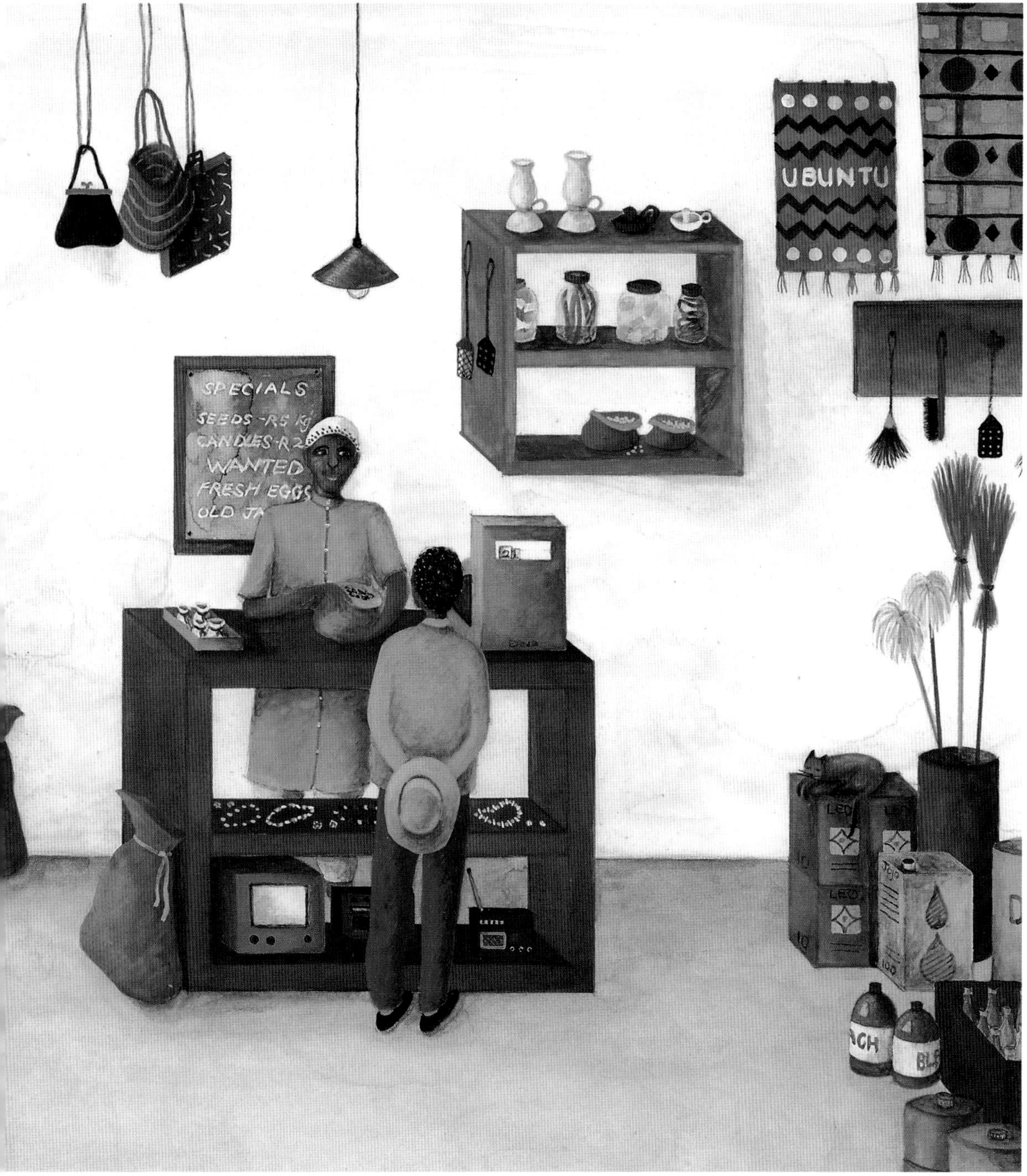

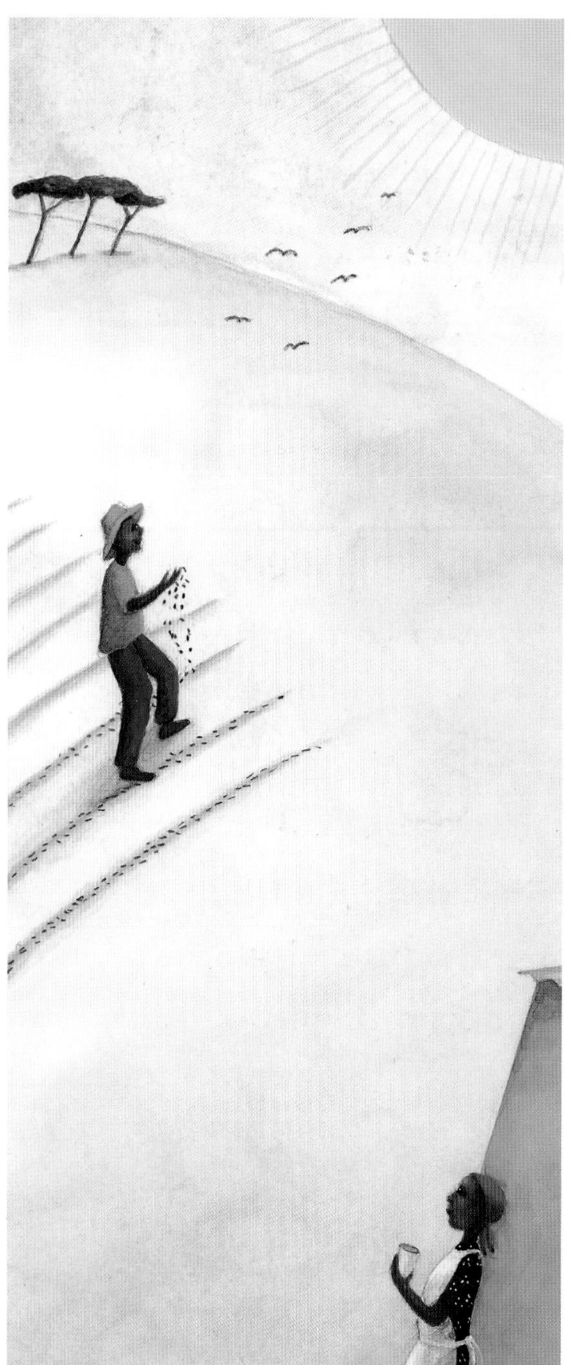

Soon the first green shoots broke through the cloddy soil. Dora weeded the field and imagined the wonderful crop they would have.

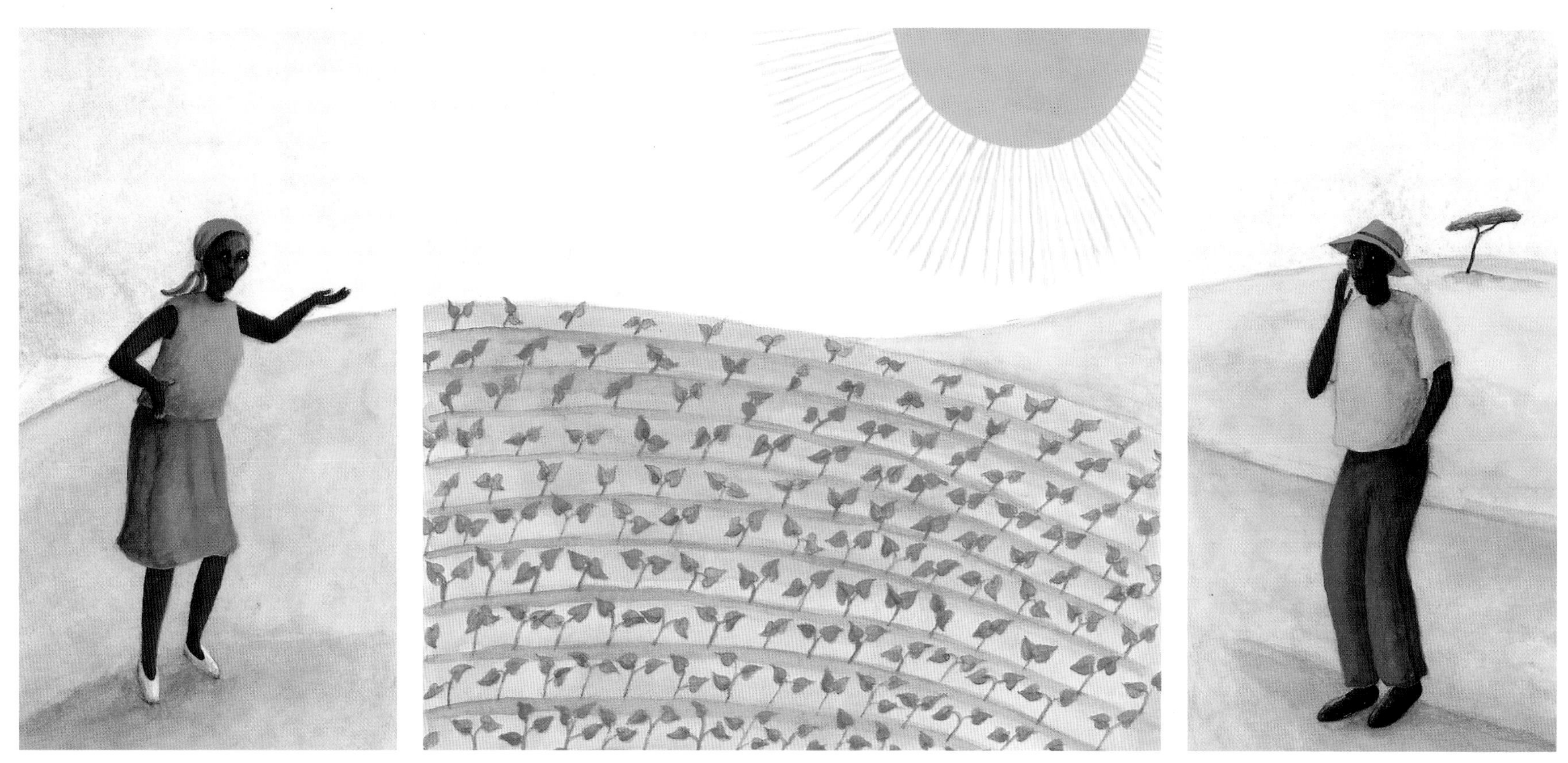

But when the leaves unfurled she came running, and cried, "Thulani, come and look! You have planted a field of sunflowers. What good are they to us? All they do is follow the sun from morning to night - just like you."

Thulani felt sad. All he wanted was to please Dora.

As the weeks passed, Thulani noticed that the sunflower heads were flopping and dropping their seeds on to the ground. There were so many seeds, he collected them in a bag and fed them to the hens.

Not long after, Dora went to collect the eggs and found two more than usual. The next day there were three more, and the following day there were eggs everywhere!

"Thulani," said Dora excitedly, "these hens are laying more eggs than ever before. They must like the sunflower seed. Now we shall have extra eggs to sell."

At last Thulani had done something right! He rushed out with the eggs, sold them at the store and bought a sheep. Late in the season, the sheep had twin lambs.

"I'm going to sell the sheep and keep the lambs," said Thulani. Dora smiled.

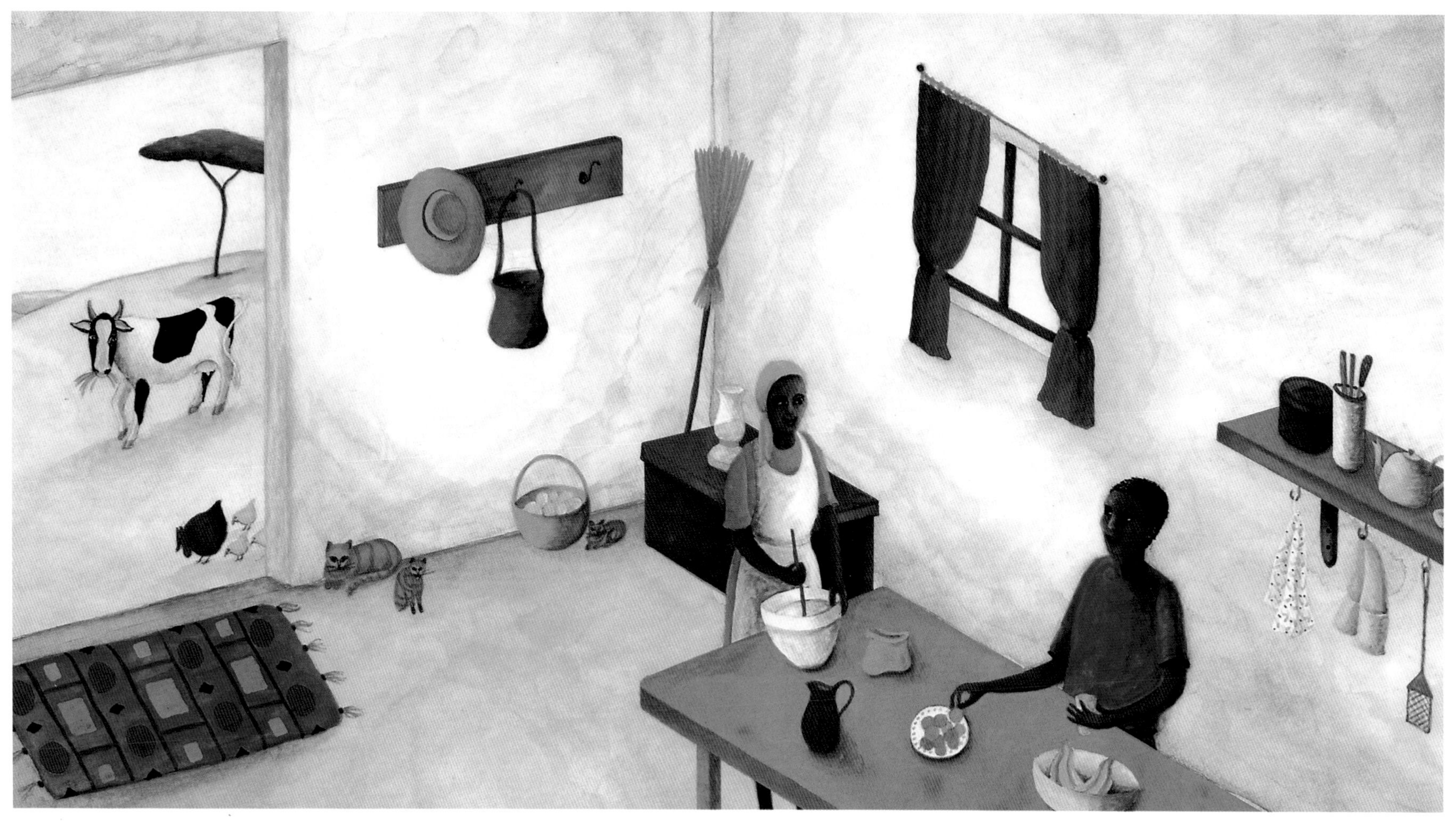

When Thulani sold the sheep and proudly brought home a cow, Dora was delighted.

"Oh Thulani! It will be good to have milk again."

Soon, Thulani became so busy trading animals, he no longer had time to sit about in the sun. Life was too exciting!

But he always found time to sit down and milk the cow.

"You know Dora, my best thoughts come to me when I'm milking," said Thulani - and they both burst out laughing, as the sun went down over the hill.

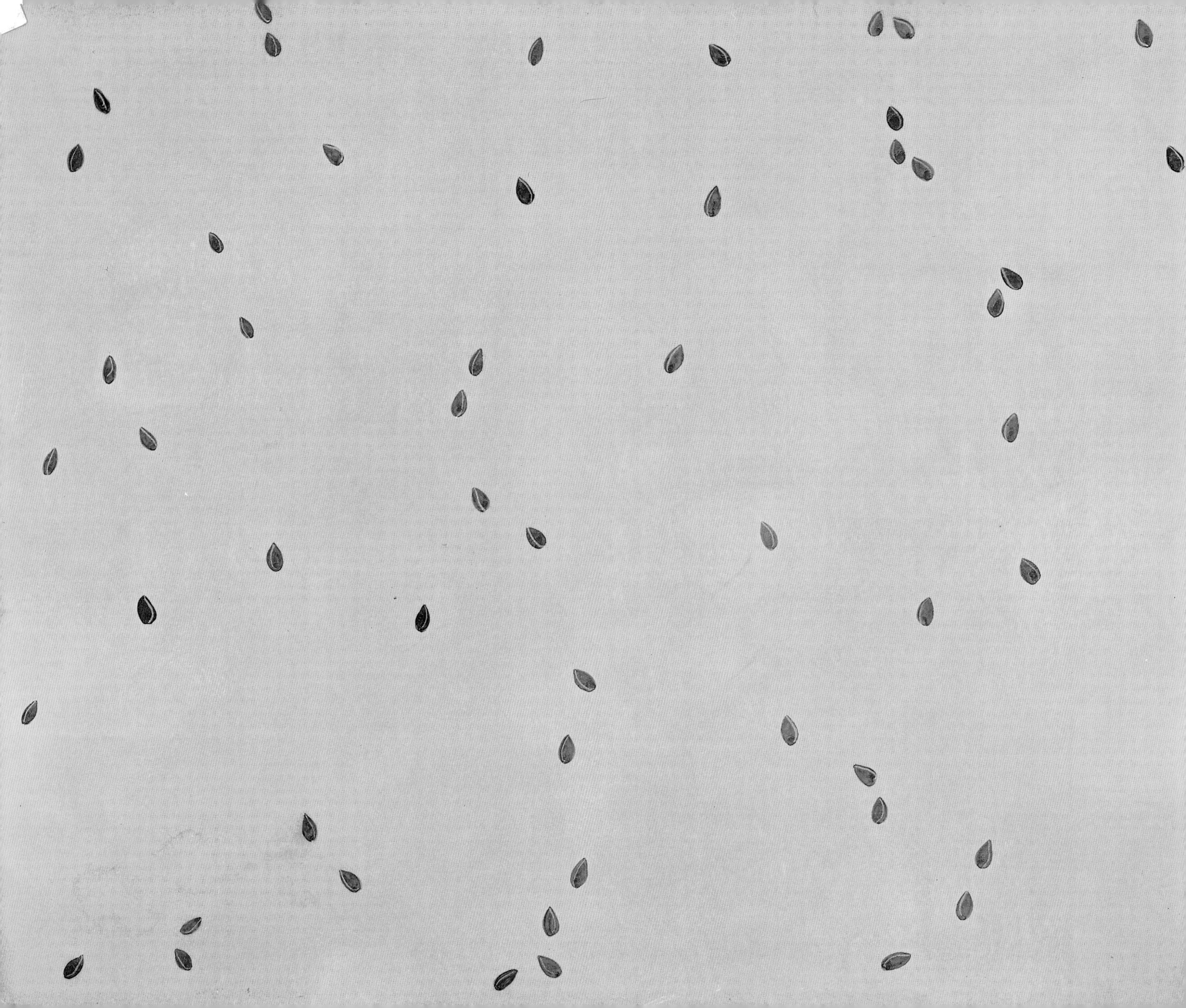

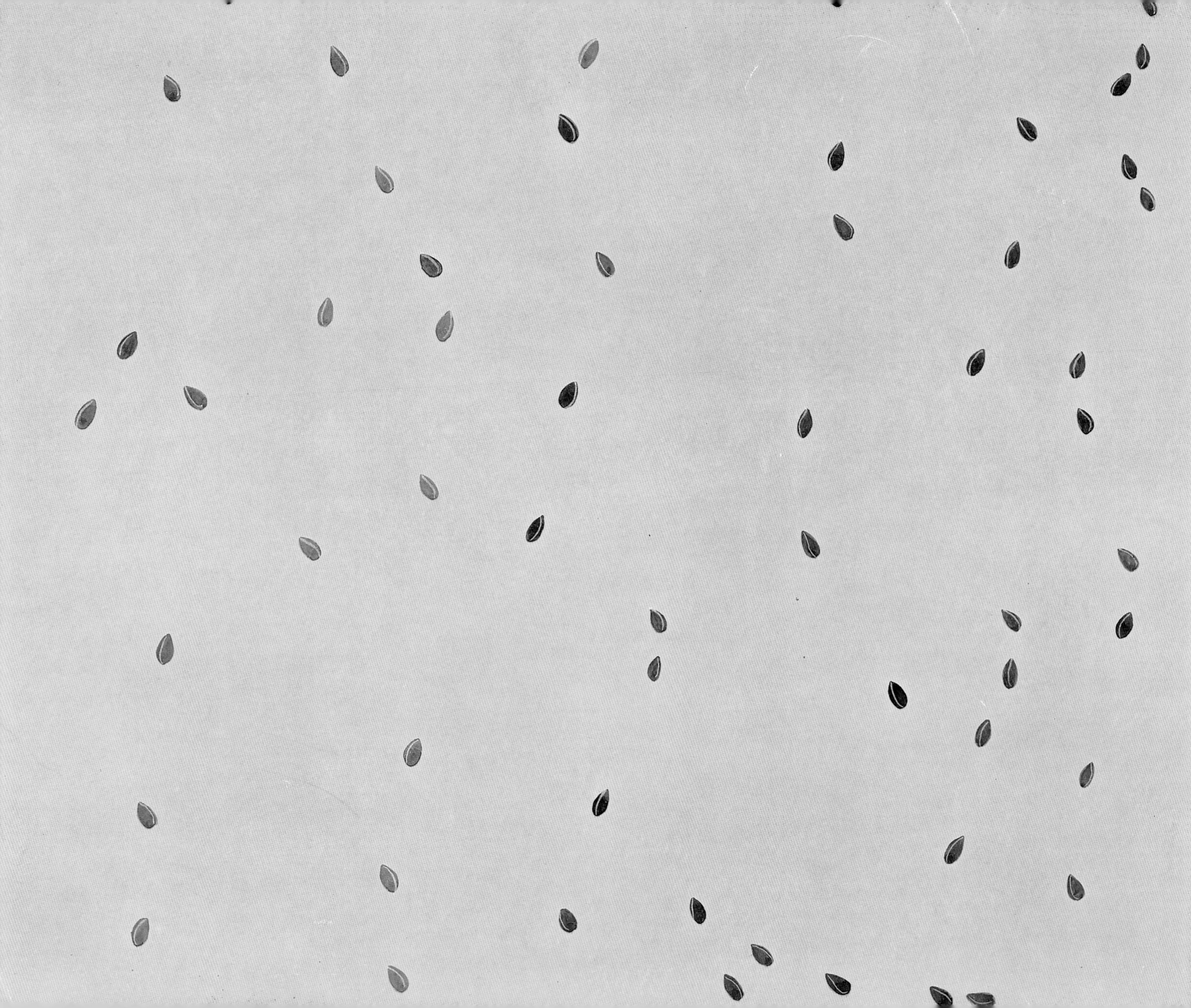

MORE TITLES FROM FRANCES LINCOLN CHILDREN'S BOOKS

The Dove

Dianne Stewart
Illustrated by Jude Daly

Waiting for the land to spring to life again after a terrible flood in the Valley of a Thousand Hills, Lindiwe and her grandmother try to earn a living selling their beautiful beadwork. Then a dove brings hope for the survivors and special good fortune for Lindiwe and her loving Gogo.

ISBN 978-1-84507-022-9

The Stone

Diane Hofmeyr
Illustrated by Jude Daly

In the Ancient Persian town of Saveh, three astronomers are gazing up at the heavens when a star like no other appears, filling the sky with fiery light. It marks the birth of a remarkable baby... Retold from an account by Marco Polo, this legend gives a fascinating perspective on the story of the Three Wise Men

ISBN 978-0-7112-1320-3 (UK)
ISBN 978-1-84507-446-7 (US)

To Every Thing There is a Season

Jude Daly

The well-loved words of Ecclesiastes take on new life and meaning in the sun-baked rural setting of a South African homestead. Jude Daly portrays an ageless world, studded with colour and miniature detail, in this very special gift book.

ISBN 978-1-884507-344-2 (UK)